I Know Sasquatch

by Jess Bradley
(and Sasquatch)

Picture Window Books

a capstone imprint

Not so long ago, I read
a book about Bigfoot.
It told me a lot of things
about this "monster" . . .

But none of those
things were true!
How did I know?

Because I've met Bigfoot!

One bright, sunny day, I was walking through the woods behind my house.

The usual suspects greeted me . . .

Then suddenly, I spotted a mysterious clump of fur.

And a large footprint!

Moments later, something moved in the bushes.

Eek! I screamed and ran.

My favorite snack spilled from my pockets . . .

... leaving a sticky sweet trail behind me.

When I finally looked back . . .

...I knew I had nothing to fear.

I was delighted to discover that
Bigfoot was quite a lovely fellow!

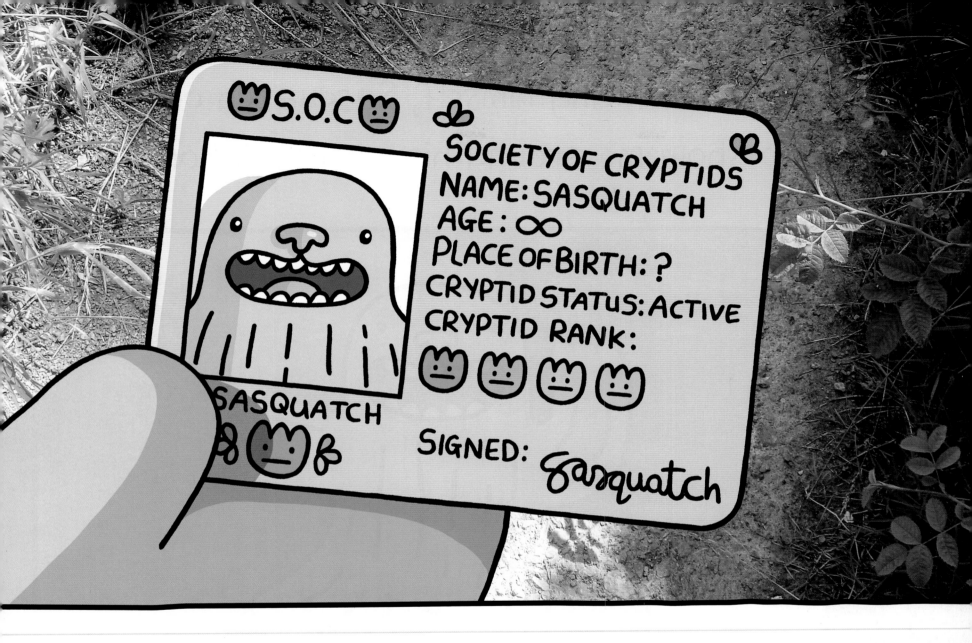

Actually, his real name is "Sasquatch."

He even proved it!

After introducing himself, Sasquatch offered
to show me around his woodland home.

First, he introduced me to his neighbors.

Then Sasquatch showed me his favorite spot.
(He likes to listen to the grasshoppers.)

We stopped there for a bit of lunch,
and Sasquatch told me about himself.

Sasquatch likes:

Video games

Teriyaki chicken

Reading comics

Toy he found
in the river

Making
decorative eggs

Watermelon

Sasquatch doesn't like:

Melty ice cream

Markers
with the cap
left off

Loud neighbors

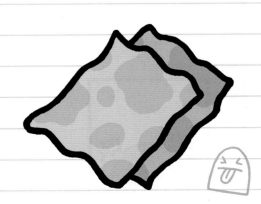

Paper-thin
ham

Angry
spiders

Plastic bags
stuck on trees
(because they look like ghosts)

Sasquatch has a family, just like you and me!

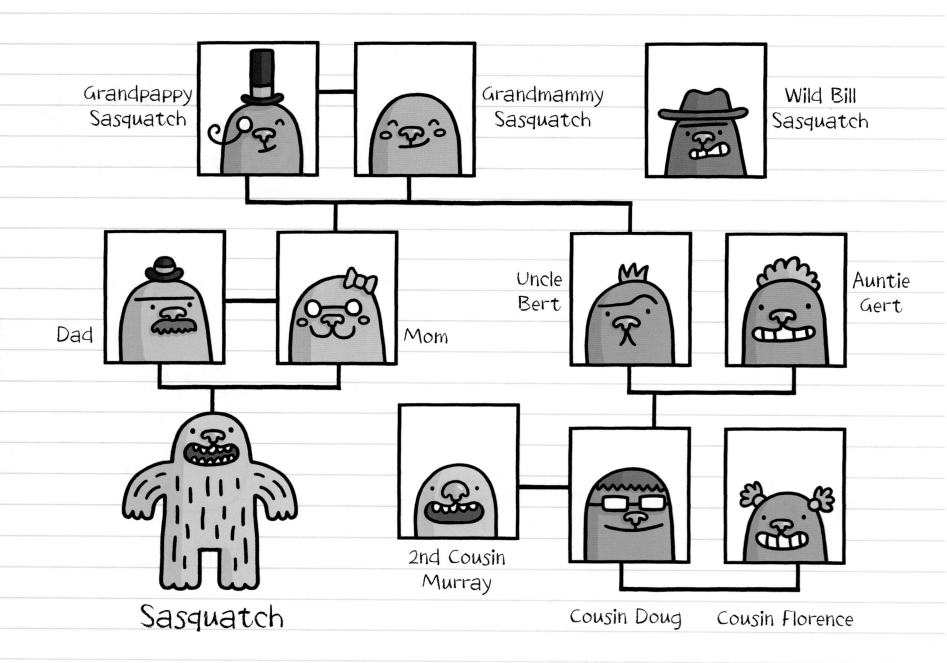

  He has many friends too!

Sasquatch really likes reading articles about himself (although nine times out of ten the stories are about his cousin, Murray).

Sasquatch really DOESN'T like photos that make him look mean (and blurry).

After a lovely day, I could finally say that I knew the REAL Sasquatch.

But one thing was bothering Sasquatch —
others still didn't know him!

There was only one thing I could do, really:

Invite him to my house
and make this book!

Now YOU know Sasquatch too!

I Know Sasquatch © 2015 by Jess Bradley

Published by Picture Window Books in 2015.

1710 Roe Crest Drive, North Mankato, MN 56003
www.mycapstone.com

Cataloging-in-Publication Data is available on the Library of Congress website.

ISBN: 978-1-4795-6481-1 (reinforced library hardcover)
ISBN: 978-1-5158-1876-2 (saddle-stitched paperback)
ISBN: 978-1-4795-8462-8 (eBook)

Book design by Bob Lentz

Printed in China.
122016   004303